For Amy, Nina, Don, Cuddles +Teh-bear

Two Bear Cubs

Ann Jonas

Greenwillow Books/New York

Printed in U.S.A. First Edition
10 9 8 7 6 5 4 3 2

Library of Congress Cataloging in Publication Data

Jonas, Ann. Two bear cubs.

Summary: Two adventurous cubs love to wander, but when frightened, appreciate having Mother close by.
[1. Bears—Fiction] I. Title.
PZ7.J664Tw   [E]   82-2860
ISBN 0-688-01407-0   AACR2
ISBN 0-688-01408-9 (lib. bdg.)

Six bright eyes look out of a dark cave.

A bear and her cubs begin their day.

The mother watches while her cubs play.

Something walks by.
It doesn't smell like a bear.

The cubs follow it.

It follows them!

**At last they outrun it.
But where are they?**

And where is their mother?

They look around.
       They sniff the ground.

No mother.

They find a honey tree all by themselves—

and a lot of angry bees!
Where is their mother?

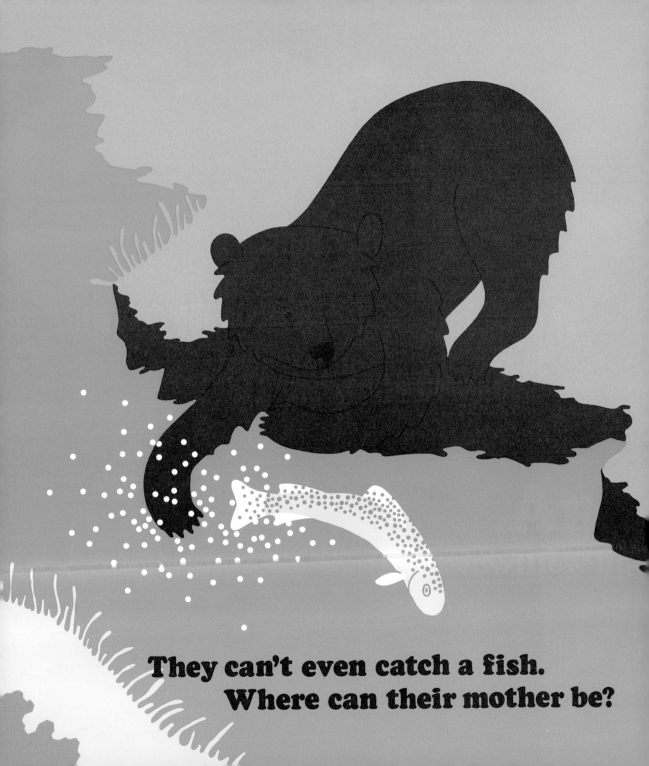

They can't even catch a fish.
Where can their mother be?

There she is!

And they aren't even very far from home.